In memory of my mother, Jennifer Gibbins,
a marvellous, magical power. And to my father, Ron Irwin,
who has been waiting till the cows come home for this.
– JI

For my little sister Shelley. You may be smaller,
but I'll always look up to you.
– CRT

First published in the United States in 2019 by Sourcebooks Kids

Text © 2018, 2019 by Jonathan Irwin
Illustrations © 2018, 2019 by Chris "Roy" Taylor
Design and editing © 2018 Lake Press Pty Ltd.

Published by Sourcebooks Jabberwocky, an imprint of
Sourcebooks Kids
P.O. Box 4410, Naperville, Illinois 60567–4410
(630) 961-3900
sourcebookskids.com

Originally published in 2018 in Australia by Lake Press Pty Ltd.
Library of Congress Cataloging-in-Publication Data is on file with
the publisher.

Source of Production: Wa Fai Printing & Paper Product
(Shenzhen) Co., Ltd
Date of Production: June 2019
Run Number: LP19 267
Printed and bound in China.
10 9 8 7 6 5 4 3 2 1

HOW TO SPEAK
COW

BY JONATHAN IRWIN
ILLUSTRATED BY CHRIS "ROY" TAYLOR

sourcebooks
jabberwocky

"MOO" means they don't.

"MOO" means they'll miss you.

"MOO" means they won't.

"MOO" means,
"My grass is tasty.
Please give it a try."

"MOO" means "horn."

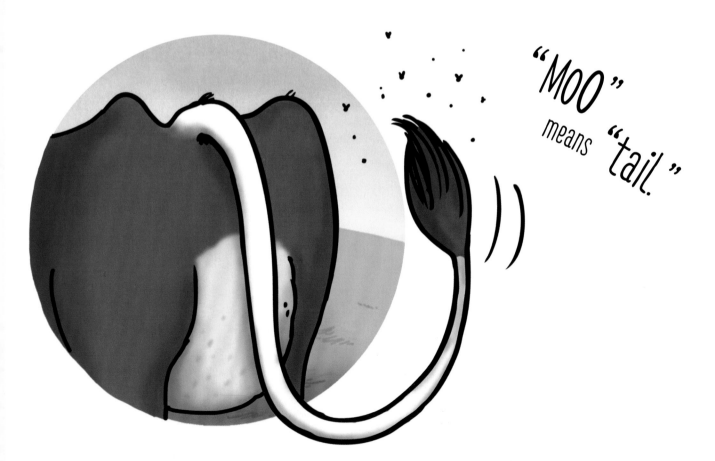

"MOO" means "tail."

"MOO" means "shed."

"MOO" means "sty."

"MOO" means, "The henhouse is so good for staying dry."

"MOO"
means,
"I'm happy."

"MOO"
means,
"I'm sad."

"MOO" means,
"Let's drive around like
racecar drivers do!"

"MOO" means "go."

"MOO" means "stop."

"MOO" means,
"I love to juggle hens until they drop."

"MOO" means "left," "right,"

"back,"   and   "straight ahead."

"MOO" means, "We need your help—
where are you? Please be quick!
We need you now to chase away the
scarecrow with your stick!"

So if you ever meet a cow
who gives that frightened "MOO,"
I hope that you'll be very brave,
and that's what you will do.

BUT if ever—if ever—a cow tells you this:
"My mind is a marvelous, magical **power**
that roams round the universe hour by **hour**.

It skips along moonbeams and bounces off **stars**.

It flips over Saturn and dances on **Mars**..."